A Porcupine in a Pine Tree

A Canadian 12 Days of Christmas

Helaine Becker

illustrated by
Werner Zimmermann

North Winds Press
An Imprint of Scholastic Canada Ltd.

The paintings for this book were created in pencil, ink and watercolour on Arches 90lb hot press paper.

www.scholastic.ca

Library and Archives Canada Cataloguing in Publication
Becker, Helaine, 1961-
A porcupine in a pine tree : a Canadian 12 days of
Christmas / Helaine Becker ; illustrated by Werner
Zimmermann.

ISBN 978-0-545-98663-2

1. Christmas--Juvenile poetry. 2. Canada--Juvenile poetry.
I. Zimmermann, Werner II. Title.

PS8553.E295532P67 2010   jC811'.6   C2010-902623-3

6 5 4 3 2 1   Printed in Singapore 46   10 11 12 13 14

*To the greatest kids
in the world — Canadian kids!*
❧ H.B.

From a loving Grumpa to his darling Blipette.
❧ W.Z.

On the first day of Christmas,
My true love gave to me:
A porcupine in a pine tree.

On the second day of Christmas,
My true love gave to me:
Two caribou,
And a porcupine in a pine tree.

On the third day of Christmas,
My true love gave to me:
Three beaver tails,
Two caribou,
And a porcupine in a pine tree.

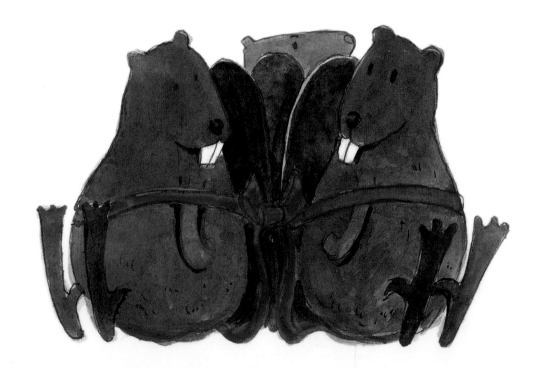

On the fourth day of Christmas,
My true love gave to me:
Four calling moose,
Three beaver tails,
Two caribou,
And a porcupine in a pine tree.

On the fifth day of Christmas,
My true love gave to me:
Five Stanley Cups,
Four calling moose,
Three beaver tails,
Two caribou,
And a porcupine in a pine tree.

On the sixth day of Christmas,
My true love gave to me:
Six squirrels curling,
Five Stanley Cups,
Four calling moose,
Three beaver tails,
Two caribou,
And a porcupine in a pine tree.

On the seventh day of Christmas,
My true love gave to me:

Seven sled dogs sledding,
Six squirrels curling,
Five Stanley Cups,
Four calling moose,
Three beaver tails,
Two caribou,
And a porcupine in a pine tree.

On the eighth day of Christmas,
My true love gave to me:
Eight Mounties munching,
Seven sled dogs sledding,
Six squirrels curling,
Five Stanley Cups,
Four calling moose,
Three beaver tails,
Two caribou,
And a porcupine in a pine tree.

On the ninth day of Christmas,
My true love gave to me:

Nine loons canoeing,
Eight Mounties munching,
Seven sled dogs sledding,
Six squirrels curling,
Five Stanley Cups,
Four calling moose,
Three beaver tails,
Two caribou,
And a porcupine in a pine tree.

On the tenth day of Christmas,
My true love gave to me:
Ten Leafs a-leaping,
Nine loons canoeing,
Eight Mounties munching,
Seven sled dogs sledding,
Six squirrels curling,
Five Stanley Cups,
Four calling moose,
Three beaver tails,
Two caribou,
And a porcupine in a pine tree.

On the eleventh day of Christmas,
My true love gave to me:
Eleven puffins piping,
Ten Leafs a-leaping,
Nine loons canoeing,
Eight Mounties munching,
Seven sled dogs sledding,
Six squirrels curling,
Five Stanley Cups,
Four calling moose,
Three beaver tails,
Two caribou,
And a porcupine in a pine tree.

On the twelfth day of Christmas,
My true love gave to me:
Twelve cubs a-dancing,
Eleven puffins piping,
Ten Leafs a-leaping,
Nine loons canoeing,
Eight Mounties munching,
Seven sled dogs sledding,
Six squirrels curling,
Five Stanley Cups,
Four calling moose,
Three beaver tails,
Two caribou . . .

And a porcupine . . .

. . . in a . . .

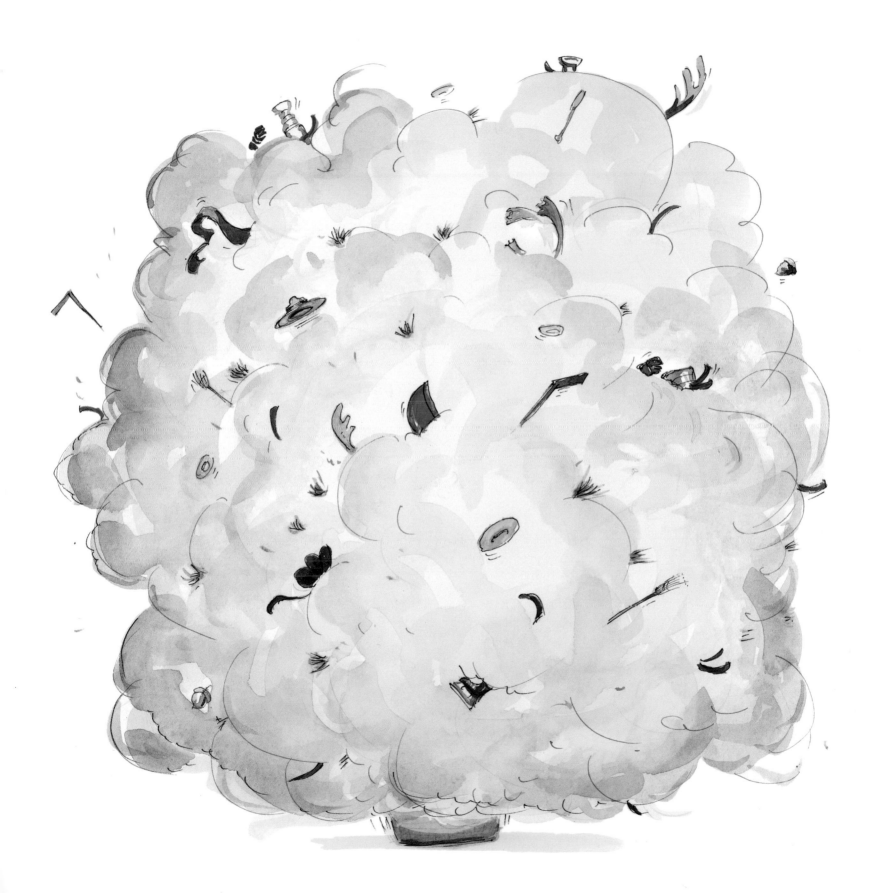

PINE TREE!

Timothy Tugbottom Says No!

By ANNE TYLER

Illustrated by MITRA MODARRESSI

G. P. PUTNAM'S SONS · NEW YORK

G. P. PUTNAM'S SONS
A division of Penguin Young Readers Group
Published by The Penguin Group
Penguin Group (USA) Inc., 375 Hudson Street, New York, NY 10014, U.S.A.
Penguin Group (Canada), 10 Alcorn Avenue, Toronto, Ontario, Canada M4V 3B2 (a division of Pearson Penguin Canada Inc.)
Penguin Books Ltd, 80 Strand, London WC2R 0RL, England.
Penguin Ireland, 25 St. Stephen's Green, Dublin 2, Ireland (a division of Penguin Books Ltd.)
Penguin Group (Australia), 250 Camberwell Road, Camberwell, Victoria 3124, Australia (a division of Pearson Australia Group Pty Ltd).
Penguin Books India Pvt Ltd, 11 Community Centre, Panchsheel Park, New Delhi - 110 017, India.
Penguin Group (NZ), Cnr Airborne and Rosedale Roads, Albany, Auckland 1310, New Zealand (a division of Pearson New Zealand Ltd).
Penguin Books (South Africa) (Pty) Ltd, 24 Sturdee Avenue, Rosebank, Johannesburg 2196, South Africa.
Penguin Books Ltd, Registered Offices: 80 Strand, London WC2R 0RL, England.

Published simultaneously in Canada. Manufactured in China by South China Printing Co. Ltd.
Design by Marikka Tamura. Text set in Badger Medium.
The art was done on Fabriano hot press watercolor paper with Winsor & Newton watercolors.
Library of Congress Cataloging-in-Publication Data
Tyler, Anne. Timothy Tugbottom says no! / by Anne Tyler ; illustrated by Mitra Modarressi. p. cm.
Summary: Timothy Tugbottom likes his old pants, his old crib, his old bedtime story, and his old breakfast,
until he realizes that new things, including sleepovers, can be good too.
[1. Change — Fiction.] I. Modarressi, Mitra, ill. II. Title.
PZ7.T937Tim 2005   [E] — dc22   2004028094   ISBN 0-399-24255-4
1 3 5 7 9 10 8 6 4 2
First Impression

For Taghi Jon and Dorri June,
with love from both of us

Timothy Tugbottom had a pair of faded pants that he wore every single day when they weren't in the wash.

One Saturday morning, his mother said, "Wouldn't you like to put on these new pants I bought you?"

But Timothy said, "No! No! No! I don't want to wear those!"

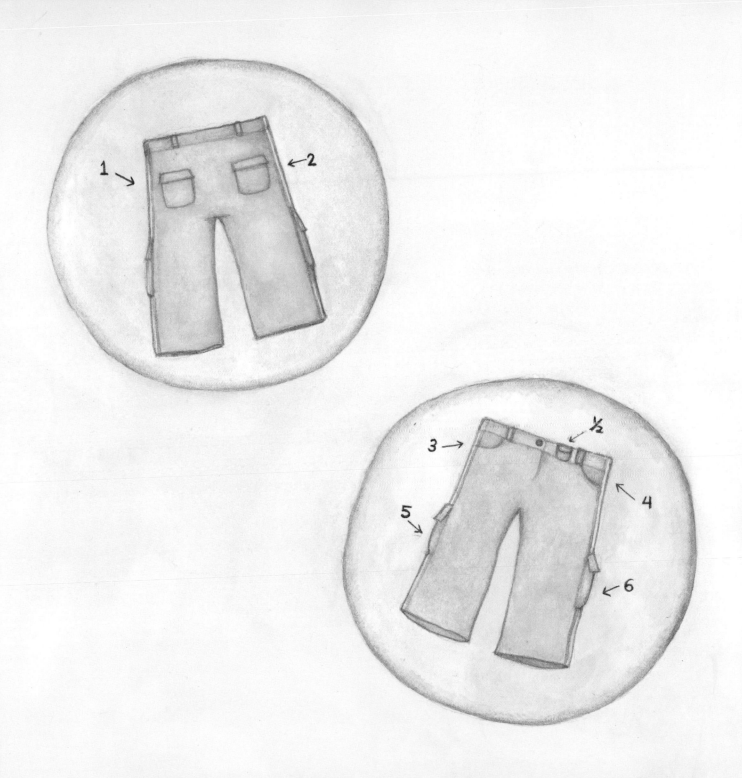

Even though the new pants had six and a half pockets.

Timothy Tugbottom liked to eat Zappos for breakfast.

One Saturday morning, when
his mother offered him a muffin,
Timothy said, "No! No! No!
I don't want to eat that!"

Even though the muffin
had blueberries in it.

Timothy Tugbottom went to school every weekday with his two best friends, Polly Peartree and Bobby Bagel.

But one Saturday, when Polly Peartree had a birthday party, Timothy said, "No! No! No! I don't want to go to a party!"

Even though Polly's cake had candles
that sparkled like firecrackers.

Timothy Tugbottom
liked to read
A Is for Anything
every night before
bedtime.

One Saturday night,
when his mother
brought out the
new book his
grandma had sent
him, Timothy said,
"No! No! No!
I don't want to read
a different book!"

Even though this was
a book about dinosaurs.

Timothy Tugbottom liked to sleep in his warm, safe crib.

One Saturday night, when his father showed him his new big-boy bed, Timothy said, "No! No! No! I don't want to sleep in a different bed!"

Even though the big-boy bed had another bed underneath
so that he could have a friend spend the night.

And he tried to stretch his arms out, but they were too long, and he tried to straighten his legs out, but his feet hit the footboard.

He said, "I'm getting too BIG for this bed!"

It was not an easy night.

The next morning, Timothy Tugbottom got up and tried
his new pants on. They had nice long legs, and he
could fit all his favorite things into the pockets.

For breakfast he had Zappos, and two bites of a muffin
with big, fat, juicy blueberries in it.

And in the afternoon he went to Bobby Bagel's birthday party, where he played running games and hiding games and ate three pieces of cake.

But when Bobby Bagel asked
him if he'd like to sleep over,
Timothy Tugbottom said,
"Oh, well, maybe tomorrow
I'll try that."

And then he went home with his mother and father, and
that night his mother read him his new dinosaur book . . .

. . . and his father tucked him into his big-boy bed,
which was very, very comfortable.